Edmund Henry Garrett

Snow Bound

A Winter Idyl

Edmund Henry Garrett

Snow Bound
A Winter Idyl

ISBN/EAN: 9783337255176

Printed in Europe, USA, Canada, Australia, Japan

Cover: Foto ©Andreas Hilbeck / pixelio.de

More available books at **www.hansebooks.com**

SNOW-BOUND

A WINTER IDYL BY
JOHN GREENLEAF WHITTIER
WITH DESIGNS BY
E H GARRETT

BOSTON AND NEW YORK
HOUGHTON, MIFFLIN AND COMPANY
The Riverside Press, Cambridge
M DCCC XCII

The Riverside Press, Cambridge, Mass., U. S. A.
Electrotyped and Printed by H. O. Houghton & Co.

TO THE MEMORY

OF

THE HOUSEHOLD IT DESCRIBES

𝕮𝖍𝖎𝖘 𝕻𝖔𝖊𝖒 𝖎𝖘 𝕯𝖊𝖉𝖎𝖈𝖆𝖙𝖊𝖉

BY

THE AUTHOR

HE inmates of the family at the Whittier homestead who are referred to in the poem were my father, mother, my brother and two sisters, and my uncle and aunt both unmarried. In addition, there was the district school-master who boarded with us. The "not unfeared, half-welcome guest" was Harriet Livermore, daughter of Judge Livermore, of New Hampshire, a young woman of fine natural ability, enthusiastic, eccentric, with slight control over her violent temper, which sometimes made her religious profession doubtful. She was equally ready to exhort in school-house prayer-meetings and dance in a Washington ball-room, while her father was a member of Congress. She early embraced the doctrine of the Second Advent, and felt it her duty to proclaim the

Lord's speedy coming. With this message she crossed the Atlantic and spent the greater part of a long life in travelling over Europe and Asia. She lived some time with Lady Hester Stanhope, a woman as fantastic and mentally strained as herself, on the slope of Mt. Lebanon, but finally quarrelled with her in regard to two white horses with red marks on their backs which suggested the idea of saddles, on which her titled hostess expected to ride into Jerusalem with the Lord. A friend of mine found her, when quite an old woman, wandering in Syria with a tribe of Arabs, who with the Oriental notion that madness is inspiration, accepted her as their prophetess and leader. At the time referred to in *Snow-Bound* she was boarding at the Rocks Village about two miles from us.

In my boyhood, in our lonely farm-house, we had scanty sources of information; few books and only a small weekly newspaper. Our only annual was the Almanac. Under such circumstances story-telling was a neces-

sary resource in the long winter evenings. My father when a young man had traversed the wilderness to Canada, and could tell us of his adventures with Indians and wild beasts, and of his sojourn in the French villages. My uncle was ready with his record of hunting and fishing and, it must be confessed, with stories which he at least half believed, of witchcraft and apparitions. My mother, who was born in the Indian-haunted region of Somerworth, New Hampshire, between Dover and Portsmouth, told us of the inroads of the savages, and the narrow escape of her ancestors. She described strange people who lived on the Piscataqua and Cocheco, among whom was Bantam the sorcerer. I have in my possession the wizard's " conjuring book," which he solemnly opened when consulted. It is a copy of Cornelius Agrippa's *Magic* printed in 1651, dedicated to Dr. Robert Child, who, like Michael Scott, had learned

> " the art of glammorie
> In Padua beyond the sea,"

and who is famous in the annals of Massachusetts, where he was at one time a resident, as the first man who dared petition the General Court for liberty of conscience. The full title of the book is *Three Books of Occult Philosophy, by Henry Cornelius Agrippa, Knight, Doctor of both Laws, Counsellor to Cæsar's Sacred Majesty and Judge of the Prerogative Court.*

J. G. W.

List of Illustrations

The Photogravures were executed by A. W. Elson & Co., Boston.

" As the Spirits of Darkness be stronger in the dark, so Good Spirits, which be Angels of Light, are augmented not only by the Divine light of the Sun, but also by our common VVood Fire : and as the Celestial Fire drives away dark spirits, so also this our Fire of VVood doth the same." — COR. AGRIPPA, *Occult Philosophy*, Book I. ch. v.

" Announced by all the trumpets of the sky,
    Arrives the snow, and, driving o'er the fields,
    Seems nowhere to alight : the whited air
    Hides hills and woods, the river and the heaven,
    And veils the farm-house at the garden's end.
    The sled and traveller stopped, the courier's feet
    Delayed, all friends shut out, the housemates sit
    Around the radiant fireplace, enclosed
    In a tumultuous privacy of storm."
                    EMERSON.   *The Snow Storm.*

Snow-Bound: A Winter Idyl

THE sun that brief December day
Rose cheerless over hills of gray,
And darkly circled, gave at noon
A sadder light than waning moon.
Slow tracing down the thickening sky
Its mute and ominous prophecy,
A portent seeming less than threat,
It sank from sight before it set.
A chill no coat, however stout,
Of homespun stuff could quite shut out,
A hard, dull bitterness of cold,
That checked, mid-vein, the circling race
Of life blood in the sharpened face,

1

The coming of the snow-storm told.
The wind blew east ; we heard the roar
Of Ocean on his wintry shore,
And felt the strong pulse throbbing there
Beat with low rhythm our inland air.

MEANWHILE we did our nightly
  chores, —
Brought in the wood from out of doors,
Littered the stalls, and from the mows
Raked down the herd's-grass for the cows :
Heard the horse whinnying for his corn ;
And, sharply clashing horn on horn,
Impatient down the stanchion rows
The cattle shake their walnut bows ;
While, peering from his early perch
Upon the scaffold's pole of birch,
The cock his crested helmet bent
And down his querulous challenge sent.

U NWARMED by any sunset light,
 The gray day darkened into night,
A night made hoary with the swarm
And whirl-dance of the blinding storm,
As zigzag, wavering to and fro,
Crossed and recrossed the wingëd snow :
And ere the early bedtime came
The white drift piled the window-frame,
And through the glass the clothes-line
 posts
Looked in like tall and sheeted ghosts.

S O all night long the storm roared on :
 The morning broke without a sun ;
In tiny spherule traced with lines
Of Nature's geometric signs,
In starry flake, and pellicle,
All day the hoary meteor fell ;
And, when the second morning shone,
We looked upon a world unknown,

3

On nothing we could call our own.
Around the glistening wonder bent
The blue walls of the firmament,
No cloud above, no earth below, —
A universe of sky and snow !
The old familiar sights of ours
Took marvellous shapes ; strange domes
        and towers
Rose up where sty or corn-crib stood,
Or garden-wall, or belt of wood ;
A smooth white mound the brush-pile
        showed,
A fenceless drift what once was road ;
The bridle-post an old man sat
With loose-flung coat and high cocked hat ;
The well-curb had a Chinese roof ;
And even the long sweep, high aloof,
In its slant splendor, seemed to tell
Of Pisa's leaning miracle.

A PROMPT, decisive man, no breath
Our father wasted : " Boys, a path ! "
Well pleased, (for when did farmer boy
Count such a summons less than joy ?)
Our buskins on our feet we drew ;
With mittened hands, and caps drawn low,
To guard our necks and ears from snow,
We cut the solid whiteness through.
And, where the drift was deepest, made
A tunnel walled and overlaid
With dazzling crystal : we had read
Of rare Aladdin's wondrous cave,
And to our own his name we gave,
With many a wish the luck were ours
To test his lamp's supernal powers.
We reached the barn with merry din,
And roused the prisoned brutes within.
The old horse thrust his long head out,
And grave with wonder gazed about ;
The cock his lusty greeting said,

And forth his speckled harem led ;
The oxen lashed their tails, and hooked,
And mild reproach of hunger looked ;
The hornëd patriarch of the sheep,
Like Egypt's Amun roused from sleep,
Shook his sage head with gesture mute,
And emphasized with stamp of foot.

ALL day the gusty north-wind bore
The loosening drift its breath be-
fore ;
Low circling round its southern zone,
The sun through dazzling snow-mist shone.
No church-bell lent its Christian tone
To the savage air, no social smoke
Curled over woods of snow-hung oak.
A solitude made more intense
By dreary-voicëd elements,
The shrieking of the mindless wind,
The moaning tree-boughs swaying blind,
And on the glass the unmeaning beat

6

Of ghostly finger-tips of sleet.
Beyond the circle of our hearth
No welcome sound of toil or mirth
Unbound the spell, and testified
Of human life and thought outside.
We minded that the sharpest ear
The buried brooklet could not hear,
The music of whose liquid lip
Had been to us companionship,
And, in our lonely life, had grown
To have an almost human tone.

A S night drew on, and, from the crest
Of wooded knolls that ridged the
west,
The sun, a snow-blown traveller, sank
From sight beneath the smothering bank,
We piled, with care, our nightly stack
Of wood against the chimney-back, —
The oaken log, green, huge, and thick,
And on its top the stout back-stick ;

The knotty forestick laid apart,
And filled between with curious art
The ragged brush ; then, hovering near,
We watched the first red blaze appear,
Heard the sharp crackle, caught the gleam
On whitewashed wall and sagging beam,
Until the old, rude-furnished room
Burst, flower-like, into rosy bloom ;
While radiant with a mimic flame
Outside the sparkling drift became,
And through the bare-boughed lilac-tree
Our own warm hearth seemed blazing free.
The crane and pendent trammels showed,
The Turks' heads on the andirons glowed ;
While childish fancy, prompt to tell
The meaning of the miracle,
Whispered the old rhyme : " *Under the tree,*
When fire outdoors burns merrily,
There the witches are making tea."

8

THE moon above the eastern wood
        Shone at its full; the hill-range
            stood
Transfigured in the silver flood,
Its blown snows flashing cold and keen,
Dead white, save where some sharp ravine
Took shadow, or the sombre green
Of hemlocks turned to pitchy black
Against the whiteness at their back.
For such a world and such a night
Most fitting that unwarming light,
Which only seemed where'er it fell
To make the coldness visible.

SHUT in from all the world without,
        We sat the clean-winged hearth
            about,
Content to let the north-wind roar
In baffled rage at pane and door,
While the red logs before us beat

The frost-line back with tropic heat;
And ever, when a louder blast
Shook beam and rafter as it passed,
The merrier up its roaring draught
The great throat of the chimney laughed;
The house-dog on his paws outspread
Laid to the fire his drowsy head,
The cat's dark silhouette on the wall
A couchant tiger's seemed to fall;
And, for the winter fireside meet,
Between the andirons' straddling feet,
The mug of cider simmered slow,
The apples sputtered in a row,
And, close at hand, the basket stood
With nuts from brown October's wood.

WHAT matter how the night be-
haved?
What matter how the north-wind raved?
Blow high, blow low, not all its snow
Could quench our hearth-fire's ruddy glow.

10

O Time and Change ! — with hair as gray
As was my sire's that winter day,
How strange it seems, with so much gone
Of life and love, to still live on !
Ah, brother ! only I and thou
Are left of all that circle now, —
The dear home faces whereupon
That fitful firelight paled and shone.
Henceforward, listen as we will,
The voices of that hearth are still ;
Look where we may, the wide earth o'er
Those lighted faces smile no more.
We tread the paths their feet have worn,
   We sit beneath their orchard trees,
   We hear, like them, the hum of bees,
And rustle of the bladed corn ;
We turn the pages that they read,
   Their written words we linger o'er,
But in the sun they cast no shade,
No voice is heard, no sign is made,
   No step is on the conscious floor !

11

Yet Love will dream, and Faith will trust,
(Since He who knows our need is just,)
That somehow, somewhere, meet we must.
Alas for him who never sees
The stars shine through his cypress-trees !
Who, hopeless, lays his dead away,
Nor looks to see the breaking day
Across the mournful marbles play !
Who hath not learned, in hours of faith,
    The truth to flesh and sense unknown,
That Life is ever lord of Death,
    And Love can never lose its own !

WE sped the time with stories old,
        Wrought puzzles out, and riddles
            told,
Or stammered from our school-book lore
" The Chief of Gambia's golden shore."
How often since, when all the land
Was clay in Slavery's shaping hand,
As if a far-blown trumpet stirred

The languorous sin-sick air, I heard :
" *Does not the voice of reason cry,*
  Claim the first right which Nature gave,
From the red scourge of bondage fly,
  Nor deign to live a burdened slave ! "
Our father rode again his ride
On Memphremagog's wooded side ;
Sat down again to moose and samp
In trapper's hut and Indian camp ;
Lived o'er the old idyllic ease
Beneath St. François' hemlock-trees ;
Again for him the moonlight shone
On Norman cap and bodiced zone ;
Again he heard the violin play
Which led the village dance away,
And mingled in its merry whirl
The grandam and the laughing girl.
Or, nearer home, our steps he led
Where Salisbury's level marshes spread
  Mile-wide as flies the laden bee ;
Where merry mowers, hale and strong,

13

Swept, scythe on scythe, their swaths
    along
  The low green prairies of the sea.
We shared the fishing off Boar's Head,
  And round the rocky Isles of Shoals
  The hake-broil on the drift-wood coals ;
The chowder on the sand-beach made,
Dipped by the hungry, steaming hot,
With spoons of clam-shell from the pot.
We heard the tales of witchcraft old,
And dream and sigh and marvel told
To sleepy listeners as they lay
Stretched idly on the salted hay,
Adrift along the winding shores,
When favoring breezes deigned to blow
The square sail of the gundelow
And idle lay the useless oars.

OUR mother, while she turned her
    wheel
Or run the new-knit stocking-heel,

Told how the Indian hordes came down
At midnight on Cocheco town,
And how her own great-uncle bore
His cruel scalp-mark to fourscore.
Recalling, in her fitting phrase,
   So rich and picturesque and free,
   (The common unrhymed poetry
Of simple life and country ways,)
The story of her early days, —
She made us welcome to her home ;
Old hearths grew wide to give us room ;
We stole with her a frightened look
At the gray wizard's conjuring-book,
The fame whereof went far and wide
Through all the simple country side ;
We heard the hawks at twilight play,
The boat-horn on Piscataqua,
The loon's weird laughter far away ;
We fished her little trout-brook, knew
What flowers in wood and meadow grew,
What sunny hillsides autumn-brown

15

She climbed to shake the ripe nuts down,
Saw where in sheltered cove and bay
The ducks' black squadron anchored lay,
And heard the wild-geese calling loud
Beneath the gray November cloud.

THEN, haply, with a look more grave
And soberer tone, some tale she
gave
From painful Sewell's ancient tome,
Beloved in every Quaker home,
Of faith fire-wingèd by martyrdom,
Or Chalkley's Journal, old and quaint, —
Gentlest of skippers, rare sea-saint!
Who, when the dreary calms prevailed,
And water-butt and bread-cask failed,
And cruel, hungry eyes pursued
His portly presence mad for food,
With dark hints muttered under breath
Of casting lots for life or death,
Offered, if Heaven withheld supplies,

16

To be himself the sacrifice.
Then, suddenly, as if to save
The good man from his living grave,
A ripple on the water grew,
A school of porpoise flashed in view.
" Take, eat," he said, " and be content ;
These fishes in my stead are sent
By Him who gave the tangled ram
To spare the child of Abraham."

OUR uncle, innocent of books,
Was rich in lore of fields and
brooks,
The ancient teachers never dumb
Of Nature's unhoused lyceum.
In moons and tides and weather wise,
He read the clouds as prophecies,
And foul or fair could well divine,
By many an occult hint and sign,
Holding the cunning-warded keys
To all the woodcraft mysteries ;

17

Himself to Nature's heart so near
That all her voices in his ear
Of beast or bird had meanings clear,
Like Apollonius of old,
Who knew the tales the sparrows told,
Or Hermes who interpreted
What the sage cranes of Nilus said ;
Content to live where life began ;
A simple, guileless, childlike man,
Strong only on his native grounds,
The little world of sights and sounds
Whose girdle was the parish bounds,
Whereof his fondly partial pride
The common features magnified,
As Surrey hills to mountains grew
In White of Selborne's loving view, —
He told how teal and loon he shot,
And how the eagle's eggs he got,
The feats on pond and river done,
The prodigies of rod and gun ;
Till, warming with the tales he told,

Forgotten was the outside cold,
The bitter wind unheeded blew,
From ripening corn the pigeons flew,
The partridge drummed i' the wood, the
    mink
Went fishing down the river-brink.
In fields with bean or clover gay,
The woodchuck, like a hermit gray,
  Peered from the doorway of his cell ;
The muskrat plied the mason's trade,
And tier by tier his mud-walls laid ;
And from the shagbark overhead
  The grizzled squirrel dropped his shell.

NEXT, the dear aunt, whose smile of
    cheer
And voice in dreams I see and hear, —
The sweetest woman ever Fate
Perverse denied a household mate,
Who, lonely, homeless, not the less
Found peace in love's unselfishness,

And welcome wheresoe'er she went,
A calm and gracious element,
Whose presence seemed the sweet in-
    come
And womanly atmosphere of home, —
Called up her girlhood memories,
The huskings and the apple-bees,
The sleigh-rides and the summer sails,
Weaving through all the poor details
And homespun warp of circumstance
A golden woof-thread of romance.
For well she kept her genial mood
And simple faith of maidenhood ;
Before her still a cloud-land lay,
The mirage loomed across her way ;
The morning dew, that dries so soon
With others, glistened at her noon ;
Through years of toil and soil and care,
From glossy tress to thin gray hair,
All unprofaned she held apart
The virgin fancies of the heart.

20

Be shame to him of woman born
Who hath for such but thought of scorn.

THERE, too, our elder sister plied
Her evening task the stand beside ;
A full, rich nature, free to trust,
Truthful and almost sternly just,
Impulsive, earnest, prompt to act,
And make her generous thought a fact,
Keeping with many a light disguise
The secret of self-sacrifice.
O heart sore-tried! thou hast the best
That Heaven itself could give thee, — rest,
Rest from all bitter thoughts and things !
How many a poor one's blessing went
With thee beneath the low green tent
Whose curtain never outward swings !

AS one who held herself a part
Of all she saw, and let her heart
Against the household bosom lean,

21

Upon the motley-braided mat
Our youngest and our dearest sat, \
Lifting her large, sweet, asking eyes,
   Now bathed in the unfading green
And holy peace of Paradise.
Oh, looking from some heavenly hill,
   Or from the shade of saintly palms,
   Or silver reach of river calms,
Do those large eyes behold me still ?
With me one little year ago : —
The chill weight of the winter snow
   For months upon her grave has lain ;
And now, when summer south-winds blow
   And brier and harebell bloom again,
I tread the pleasant paths we trod,
I see the violet-sprinkled sod
Whereon she leaned, too frail and weak
The hillside flowers she loved to seek,
Yet following me where'er I went
With dark eyes full of love's content.
The birds are glad ; the brier-rose fills

22

The air with sweetness ; all the hills
Stretch green to June's unclouded sky ;
But still I wait with ear and eye
For something gone which should be nigh,
A loss in all familiar things,
In flower that blooms, and bird that sings.
And yet, dear heart ! remembering thee,
    Am I not richer than of old ?
Safe in thy immortality,
    What change can reach the wealth I
       hold ?
    What chance can mar the pearl and
       gold
Thy love hath left in trust with me ?
And while in life's late afternoon,
    Where cool and long the shadows grow,
I walk to meet the night that soon
    Shall shape and shadow overflow,
I cannot feel that thou art far,
Since near at need the angels are ;
And when the sunset gates unbar,

Shall I not see thee waiting stand,
And, white against the evening star,
The welcome of thy beckoning hand ?

BRISK wielder of the birch and rule,
The master of the district school
Held at the fire his favored place, \
Its warm glow lit a laughing face
Fresh-hued and fair, where scarce ap-
        peared
The uncertain prophecy of beard.
He teased the mitten-blinded cat,
Played cross-pins on my uncle's hat,
Sang songs, and told us what befalls
In classic Dartmouth's college halls.
Born the wild Northern hills among,
From whence his yeoman father wrung
By patient toil subsistence scant,
Not competence and yet not want,
He early gained the power to pay
His cheerful, self-reliant way ;

Could doff at ease his scholar's gown
To peddle wares from town to town ;
Or through the long vacation's reach
In lonely lowland districts teach,
Where all the droll experience found
At stranger hearths in boarding round,
The moonlit skater's keen delight,
The sleigh-drive through the frosty night,
The rustic party, with its rough
Accompaniment of blind-man's-buff,
And whirling plate, and forfeits paid,
His winter task a pastime made.
Happy the snow-locked homes wherein
He tuned his merry violin,
Or played the athlete in the barn,
Or held the good dame's winding-yarn,
Or mirth-provoking versions told
Of classic legends rare and old,
Wherein the scenes of Greece and Rome
Had all the commonplace of home,
And little seemed at best the odds

'Twixt Yankee pedlers and old gods ;
Where Pindus-born Arachthus took
The guise of any grist-mill brook,
And dread Olympus at his will
Became a huckleberry hill.

A CARELESS boy that night he
seemed ;
  But at his desk he had the look
And air of one who wisely schemed,
  And hostage from the future took
  In trainëd thought and lore of book.
Large-brained, clear-eyed, of such as he
Shall Freedom's young apostles be,
Who, following in War's bloody trail,
Shall every lingering wrong assail ;
All chains from limb and spirit strike,
Uplift the black and white alike ;
Scatter before their swift advance
The darkness and the ignorance,
The pride, the lust, the squalid sloth,

Which nurtured Treason's monstrous
 growth,
Made murder pastime, and the hell
Of prison-torture possible ;
The cruel lie of caste refute,
Old forms remould, and substitute
For Slavery's lash the freeman's will,
For blind routine, wise-handed skill ;
A school-house plant on every hill,
Stretching in radiate nerve-lines thence
The quick wires of intelligence ;
Till North and South together brought
Shall own the same electric thought,
In peace a common flag salute,
And, side by side in labor's free
And unresentful rivalry,
Harvest the fields wherein they fought.

ANOTHER guest that winter night
 Flashed back from lustrous eyes the
  light.

Unmarked by time, and yet not young,
The honeyed music of her tongue
And words of meekness scarcely told
A nature passionate and bold,
Strong, self-concentred, spurning guide,
Its milder features dwarfed beside
Her unbent will's majestic pride.
She sat among us, at the best,
A not unfeared, half-welcome guest,
Rebuking with her cultured phrase
Our homeliness of words and ways.
A certain pard-like, treacherous grace
  Swayed the lithe limbs and dropped the
    lash,
  Lent the white teeth their dazzling
    flash ;
  And under low brows, black with night,
  Rayed out at times a dangerous light ;
The sharp heat-lightnings of her face
Presaging ill to him whom Fate
Condemned to share her love or hate.

A woman tropical, intense
In thought and act, in soul and sense,
She blended in a like degree
The vixen and the devotee,
Revealing with each freak or feint
  The temper of Petruchio's Kate,
The raptures of Siena's saint.
Her tapering hand and rounded wrist
Had facile power to form a fist ;
The warm, dark languish of her eyes
Was never safe from wrath's surprise.
Brows saintly calm and lips devout
Knew every change of scowl and pout ;
And the sweet voice had notes more high
And shrill for social battle-cry.

SINCE then what old cathedral town
   Has missed her pilgrim staff and
      gown,
What convent-gate has held its lock
Against the challenge of her knock !

Through Smyrna's plague-hushed thor-
    oughfares,
Up sea-set Malta's rocky stairs,
Gray olive slopes of hills that hem
Thy tombs and shrines, Jerusalem,
Or startling on her desert throne
The crazy Queen of Lebanon
With claims fantastic as her own,
Her tireless feet have held their way ;
And still, unrestful, bowed, and gray,
She watches under Eastern skies,
    With hope each day renewed and fresh,
    The Lord's quick coming in the flesh,
Whereof she dreams and prophesies !

WHERE'ER her troubled path may
      be,
    The Lord's sweet pity with her go !
The outward wayward life we see,
    The hidden springs we may not know.
Nor is it given us to discern

What threads the fatal sisters spun,
Through what ancestral years has run
The sorrow with the woman born,
What forged her cruel chain of moods,
What set her feet in solitudes,
And held the love within her mute,
What mingled madness in the blood,
A life-long discord and annoy,
Water of tears with oil of joy,
And hid within the folded bud
Perversities of flower and fruit.
It is not ours to separate
The tangled skein of will and fate,
To show what metes and bounds should
      stand
Upon the soul's debatable land,
And between choice and Providence
Divide the circle of events ;
But He who knows our frame is just,
Merciful and compassionate,
And full of sweet assurances

And hope for all the language is,
That He remembereth we are dust !

A T last the great logs, crumbling low,
    Sent out a dull and duller glow,
The bull's-eye watch that hung in view,
Ticking its weary circuit through,
Pointed with mutely warning sign
Its black hand to the hour of nine.
That sign the pleasant circle broke :
My uncle ceased his pipe to smoke,
Knocked from its bowl the refuse gray,
And laid it tenderly away,
Then roused himself to safely cover
The dull red brands with ashes over.
And while, with care, our mother laid
The work aside, her steps she stayed
One moment, seeking to express
Her grateful sense of happiness
For food and shelter, warmth and health,
And love's contentment more than wealth,

With simple wishes (not the weak,
Vain prayers which no fulfilment seek,
But such as warm the generous heart,
O'er-prompt to do with Heaven its part)
That none might lack, that bitter night,
For bread and clothing, warmth and light. ,

WITHIN our beds awhile we heard
The wind that round the gables
roared,
With now and then a ruder shock,
Which made our very bedsteads rock.
We heard the loosened clapboards tost,
The board-nails snapping in the frost ;
And on us, through the unplastered wall,
Felt the light sifted snow-flakes fall.
But sleep stole on, as sleep will do
When hearts are light and life is new ;
Faint and more faint the murmurs grew,
Till in the summer-land of dreams
They softened to the sound of streams,

33

Low stir of leaves, and dip of oars,
And lapsing waves on quiet shores.

NEXT morn we wakened with the
        shout
Of merry voices high and clear;
And saw the teamsters drawing near
To break the drifted highways out.
Down the long hillside treading slow
We saw the half-buried oxen go,
Shaking the snow from heads uptost,
Their straining nostrils white with frost.
Before our door the straggling train
Drew up, an added team to gain.
The elders threshed their hands a-cold,
    Passed, with the cider-mug, their jokes
    From lip to lip; the younger folks
Down the loose snow-banks, wrestling,
        rolled,
Then toiled again the cavalcade
    O'er windy hill, through clogged ravine,

34

And woodland paths that wound be-
tween
Low drooping pine-boughs winter-weighed.
From every barn a team afoot,
At every house a new recruit,
Where, drawn by Nature's subtlest law
Haply the watchful young men saw
Sweet doorway pictures of the curls
And curious eyes of merry girls,
Lifting their hands in mock defence
Against the snow-ball's compliments,
And reading in each missive tost
The charm with Eden never lost.

WE heard once more the sleigh-bells'
sound ;
And, following where the teamsters
led,
The wise old Doctor went his round,
Just pausing at our door to say,
In the brief autocratic way

Of one who, prompt at Duty's call,
Was free to urge her claim on all,
  That some poor neighbor sick abed
At night our mother's aid would need.
For, one in generous thought and deed,
  What mattered in the sufferer's sight
  The Quaker matron's inward light,
The Doctor's mail of Calvin's creed?
All hearts confess the saints elect
  Who, twain in faith, in love agree,
And melt not in an acid sect
  The Christian pearl of charity !

S O days went on : a week had passed
    Since the great world was heard from
        last.
The Almanac we studied o'er,
Read and reread our little store
Of books and pamphlets, scarce a score ;
One harmless novel, mostly hid
From younger eyes, a book forbid,

36

And poetry, (or good or bad,
A single book was all we had,)
Where Ellwood's meek, drab-skirted Muse,
   A stranger to the heathen Nine,
   Sang, with a somewhat nasal whine,
The wars of David and the Jews.
At last the floundering carrier bore
The village paper to our door.
Lo ! broadening outward as we read,
To warmer zones the horizon spread ;
In panoramic length unrolled
We saw the marvels that it told.
Before us passed the painted Creeks,
   And daft McGregor on his raids
   In Costa Rica's everglades.
And up Taygetos winding slow
Rode Ypsilanti's Mainote Greeks,
A Turk's head at each saddle-bow !
Welcome to us its week-old news,
Its corner for the rustic Muse,
   Its monthly gauge of snow and rain,

Its record, mingling in a breath
The wedding knell and dirge of death;
Jest, anecdote, and love-lorn tale,
The latest culprit sent to jail;
Its hue and cry of stolen and lost,
Its vendue sales and goods at cost,
   And traffic calling loud for gain.
We felt the stir of hall and street,
The pulse of life that round us beat;
The chill embargo of the snow
Was melted in the genial glow;
Wide swung again our ice-locked door,
And all the world was ours once more!

CLASP, Angel of the backward look
    And folded wings of ashen gray
  And voice of echoes far away,
The brazen covers of thy book;
The weird palimpsest old and vast,
Wherein thou hid'st the spectral past;
Where, closely mingling, pale and glow

The characters of joy and woe;
The monographs of outlived years,
Or smile-illumed or dim with tears,
  Green hills of life that slope to death,
And haunts of home, whose vistaed trees
Shade off to mournful cypresses
  With the white amaranths underneath.
Even while I look, I can but heed
  The restless sands' incessant fall,
Importunate hours that hours succeed,
Each clamorous with its own sharp need,
  And duty keeping pace with all.
Shut down and clasp the heavy lids;
I hear again the voice that bids
The dreamer leave his dream midway
For larger hopes and graver fears:
Life greatens in these later years,
The century's aloe flowers to-day!

Y ET, haply, in some lull of life,
    Some Truce of God which breaks
        its strife,
The worldling's eyes shall gather dew,
    Dreaming in throngful city ways
Of winter joys his boyhood knew;
And dear and early friends — the few
Who yet remain — shall pause to view
    These Flemish pictures of old days;
Sit with me by the homestead hearth,
And stretch the hands of memory forth
    To warm them at the wood-fire's blaze!
And thanks untraced to lips unknown
Shall greet me like the odors blown
From unseen meadows newly mown,
Or lilies floating in some pond,
Wood-fringed, the wayside gaze beyond;
The traveller owns the grateful sense
Of sweetness near, he knows not whence,
And, pausing, takes with forehead bare
The benediction of the air.

Page 12. *The Chief of Gambia's golden shore.* *The African Chief* was the title of a poem by Mrs. Sarah Wentworth Morton, wife of the Hon. Perez Morton, a former attorney-general of Massachusetts. Mrs. Morton's *nom de plume* was *Philenia.* The school book in which *The African Chief* was printed was Caleb Bingham's *The American Preceptor*, and the poem contained fifteen stanzas, of which the first four were as follows : —

" See how the black ship cleaves the main
    High-bounding o'er the violet wave,
  Remurmuring with the groans of pain,
    Deep freighted with the princely slave.

" Did all the gods of Afric sleep,
    Forgetful of their guardian love,
  When the white traitors of the deep
    Betrayed him in the palmy grove ?

" A chief of Gambia's golden shore,
    Whose arm the band of warriors led,
  Perhaps the lord of boundless power,
    By whom the foodless poor were fed.

" Does not the voice of reason cry,
  ' Claim the first right which nature gave ;
  From the red scourge of bondage fly,
    Nor deign to live a burdened slave ' ? "

Page 17. *To spare the child of Abraham.*
Chalkley's own narrative of this incident, as
given in his *Journal*, is as follows : " To stop
their murmuring, I told them they should not
need to cast lots, which was usual in such
cases, which of us should die first, for I would
freely offer up my life to do them good. One
said, ' God bless you ! I will not eat any of
you.' Another said, ' He would die before he
would eat any of me ; ' and so said several. I
can truly say, on that occasion, at that time, my
life was not dear to me, and that I was serious
and ingenuous in my proposition : and as I was
leaning over the side of the vessel, thought-
fully considering my proposal to the company,

and looking in my mind to Him that made me, a very large dolphin came up towards the top or surface of the water, and looked me in the face; and I called the people to put a hook into the sea, and take him, for here is one come to redeem me (I said to them). And they put a hook into the sea, and the fish readily took it, and they caught him. He was longer than myself. I think he was about six feet long, and the largest that ever I saw. This plainly showed us that we ought not to distrust the providence of the Almighty. The people were quieted by this act of Providence, and murmured no more. We caught enough to eat plentifully of, till we got into the capes of Delaware."

Page 30. *The crazy Queen of Lebanon.* An interesting account of Lady Hester Stanhope may be found in Kinglake's *Eothen,* chapter viii.

Page 35. *The wise old Doctor went his round.* Dr. Weld of Haverhill, an old man, who died at the age of ninety-six.